# Rob Scotton

# Splat the Cat

HarperCollinsPublishers

Special thanks to Maria.

Splat the Cat

Copyright © 2008 by Rob Scotton

Printed in the U.S.A.

All rights reserved. No part of this book may be used or reproduced in any manner whatsoever
without written permission except in the case of brief quotations embodied in critical articles
and reviews. For information address HarperCollins Children's Books, a division of HarperCollins
Publishers, 1350 Avenue of the Americas, New York, NY 10019.

www.harpercollinschildrens.com

Library of Congress Cataloging-in-Publication Data is available.

ISBN 978-0-06-083154-7 (trade bdg.) — ISBN 978-0-06-083155-4 (lib. bdg.)

Typography by Neil Swaab

1 2 3 4 5 6 7 8 9 10

First Edition

For Maggie and her very own Splat cats—Spatz and Strawberry.

—R.S.

Splat

It was early in the morning
and Splat was wide awake.
Today was his first day at Cat School,
and his tail wiggled wildly with worry.

If I hide from the day, maybe *it'll go away*, he thought.

It didn't go away.

"Time to get up," said his mom.

"Time to get dressed," said his mom.

"I don't have any clean socks, Mom.
Maybe I should go to school tomorrow instead?" said Splat.

"You don't wear socks," said his mom.

"I'm having a bad hair day, Mom. Maybe I should go to school tomorrow instead?" said Splat.

His mom combed his hair. "Purr-fect!" she said.

"Don't forget your lunchbox," said his mom.

*I'll need a friend today,* thought Splat.

And he dropped his pet mouse, Seymour, into his lunchbox.

"Time to go," said his mom.

"The front door won't let me out, Mom."

"The gate won't let go of my fingers, Mom."

"The lamppost won't get out of my way, Mom."

"MOM!"

"You can ride your bike if you like, Splat," said his mom.

So he did. But he didn't say a single word.

"Welcome to Cat School," said a big, round cat.
"I'm Mrs. Wimpydimple, your teacher."

Splat's mom gave him a hug.
"I'll be back soon," she said.
"You'll be fine."

"Everyone, this is Splat.
Let's welcome him
into our class," said
Mrs. Wimpydimple.

"Hi,

Mrs. Wimpydimple began. "Cats are amazing," she said.

"We're clever, cunning, and quick."

"Am I amazing too?" asked Splat.

"Yes, you too," said Mrs. Wimpydimple.

"Cats climb trees, drink milk, and chase mice," she continued.

"Why do we chase mice?" asked Splat.
"It's what we do," replied Mrs. Wimpydimple.

"Why?" asked Splat.
"Because."

"Why?"

"Why?"

"Why?"

"Why?"

Mrs. Wimpydimple sighed.
"Lunchtime!" she announced.

Splat opened his lunchbox.

# "Mouse!"

The cats did what cats do.

Seymour hid behind a glass bottle,

and when the cats saw
his face through the glass,

they screamed and ran away.

Seymour did what
all mice want to do.

"Stop!" cried Splat.

"SPLAT!"

They didn't stop.

"Enough!" Mrs. Wimpydimple said, and it ended. "It's milk time."

"Hurray!"

But the door to the milk cupboard was stuck.
"No milk today," announced Mrs. Wimpydimple.

"AWWWW."

Splat whispered into Seymour's ear.
Seymour nodded and then . . .

A moment later,
the door swung open.

"Yum!"

Mrs. Wimpydimple wrote again on the chalkboard.

Cats don't chase mice

"Hurray!" cheered the class.

Soon it was home time.
Splat's mom returned and gave him a hug.

"I've got lots of friends. . . .

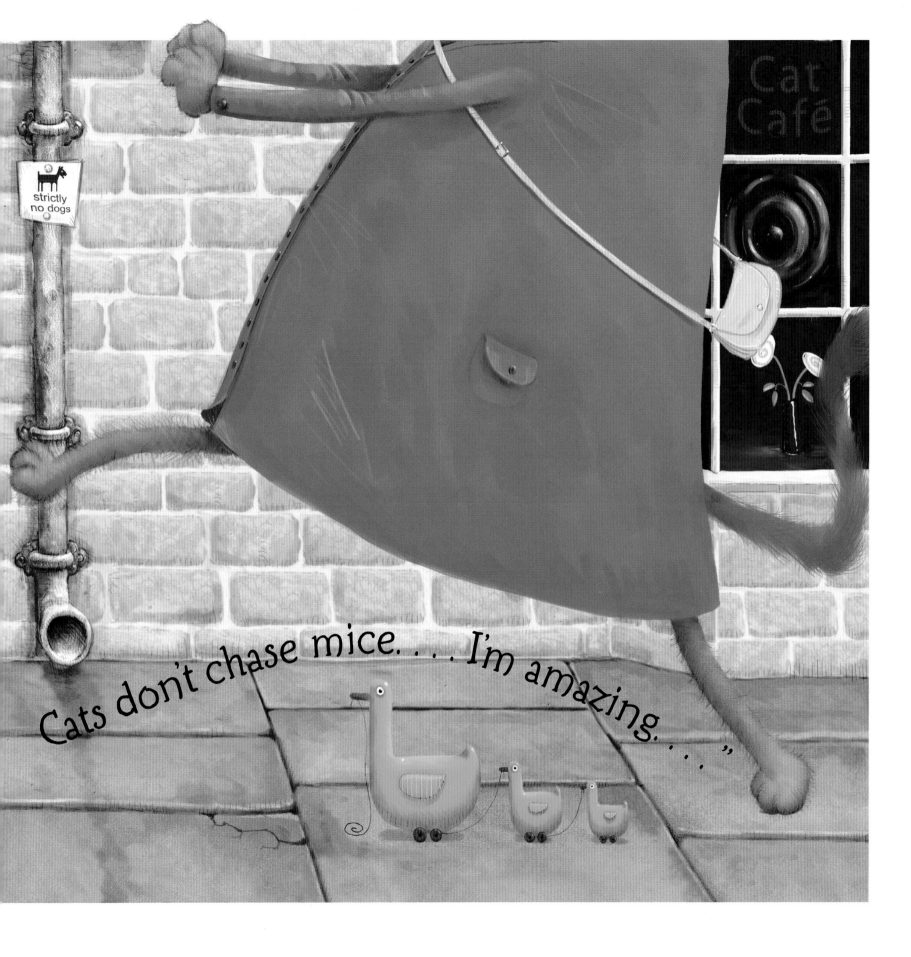

It was early the next morning
and Splat was wide awake.
Today was his second day at Cat School,
and his tail wiggled wildly . . .

. . . with excitement.

ONE SNOWY day, Charles Chinchilla was playing with his best friends, Elvis Wormly and Babs McBoid. Charles looked out the window and couldn't believe his eyes. The yard was a winter wonderland.

"I've got an idea!" he said.

"We are going to make

# THE GREATEST SNOWMAN IN THE WORLD!"

"Impossible," said Babs.

"I'm ready to wriggle!" said Elvis.

They **bounced** out the door
and
into the snow.

They rolled their snowballs **bigger** and

**bigger**

and **bigger**...

and finally stacked them into . . .

"The **worst** SNOWMAN in the **world**," said Babs.

"He just needs a nose!" said Charles.

"Who brought a carrot?" asked Elvis.

"I'VE GOT AN EVEN BETTER IDEA!" said Charles.

"This will never work," said Babs. "But I guess he could use more **eyes!**"

"More feet!" said Elvis.

"More of everything!" said Charles.

They worked
and
worked

and worked...

and finally . . .

"It's the greatest snowman in the world!"

Ker-sploit!

"Oh no! He's melting!" cried Elvis.

"We've got to save him!"

"We'll never make it!" screamed Babs.

"Ready, slingshot?!" asked Charles.

"Ready!" said Elvis.

"Okay," said Babs. "Ready . . . aim . . . "

"YES!" cheered Charles.

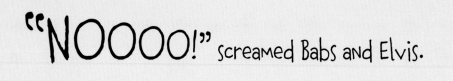

"NOOOO!" screamed Babs and Elvis.